# EGMONT

*We bring stories to life*

First published in Great Britain 2005
by Egmont Books Limited
239 Kensington High Street, London W8 6SA
Illustrated by Niall Harding
Postman Pat® © 2004 Woodland Animations Ltd,
a division of Entertainment Rights PLC
Licensed by Entertainment Rights PLC
Original writer John Cunliffe
From the original television design by Ivor Wood
Royal Mail and Post Office imagery is used
by kind permission of Royal Mail Group plc.
All rights reserved.

ISBN 1 4052 2097 X
1 3 5 7 9 10 8 6 4 2
Printed in China

# Postman Pat's
## Busy Week

PAT 1

postman
Pat

Postman Pat has a very
busy week ahead.

"Come on, Jess," he says, "Let's get
going or our work will never be done!"

"Miaow," says Jess, leaping into the van.

Mondays are always busy at the Post Office. There is a lot of sorting to do after the weekend.

"Good morning, Mrs Goggins! Hello, Dorothy!" says Postman Pat.

"Morning, Pat!" replies Mrs Goggins. "There are lots of letters for you today, as usual."

# Tuesday

On Tuesdays, Postman Pat picks up his son, Julian, from school on his way home from delivering the post. Jess likes to play with the children in the playground!

"Time to go home now, Julian," says Pat.
"And it's Tuesday today, so we're having sausages and mash for dinner!"
"Ooh, my favourite!" laughs Julian.

It's Wednesday today, which means that Ajay Bains the station master will clean The Greendale Rocket. Postman Pat calls in to the station.

"I've brought a little helper with me today," says Pat. "Charlie Pringle would like to help you clean the train."

"Wonderful!" says Ajay. "With two pairs of hands we'll have it done in no time at all!"

GREENDALE

Thursday

"Goodness me," says Pat. "It's Thursday already. The week is flying by, isn't it Jess!"

Today is a big day for Sarah Gilbertson. She's waiting for her pony club certificate after winning a competition.

"Aha!" says Pat as he arrives at the door of the clinic. "I think I might know who this is for!"

Sarah rushes happily inside to open the envelope.

Every Friday, Postman Pat collects some eggs for the weekend from Alf and Dorothy Thompson.

"Good afternoon!" says Pat.

"Oh hello, Pat!" says Dorothy. "The hens have laid some good eggs for you this week."

Pat puts the eggs carefully into the van and gets ready to set off home. But Jess is too busy chasing the hens in the field!

PAT 1

# Saturday

It's Saturday and there is a coffee morning in the church hall. Postman Pat arrives at the church with some post for Reverend Timms.

"Ah! I see you have some cakes with you today, too," says the Reverend.

"Indeed I do," smiles Pat. "Only the best — Sara baked them this morning!"

"Phew! No letters to deliver today, Jess!" says Pat.

But it is still going to be a busy day. It's Julian's birthday and they are having a party in the garden.

"Happy Birthday, Julian!" everybody sings.

Best of all, Jess can try the birthday cake.